# They Were Like Us...

## Women of the Bible

Susan Peaslee

# *Dedication*

I want to thank Carol Fulton who challenged me to write this book at one of the lowest points in my life. There were days that her challenge kept me going. Thank you to Deb Lovett for the coaching lessons. This work would not have been possible without Elin Lee's encouragement and hours of discussion and editing. Michelle Brands thank you for pushing me to the finish line. I also would be remiss not to mention the support from my family. In all honesty there are not enough words to thank all the people who have helped, supported, encouraged, prayed and listened as I read and re-read my stories to them—you know who you are. Thank you all from the bottom of my heart.

# TABLE OF CONTENTS

# FOREWORD

What you hold in your hands is not a book; it's an art form from a woman who has a creative spirit that never ends. This artwork is a *Holy Spirit-downloaded* message for all women to understand and relate with. It may bring up painful memories, but perhaps those are ones that need healing. Speaking of healing, Susan Peaslee, your creative writer of THEY WERE LIKE US, has had many painful experiences in her own life; she speaks from experience which you will come to understand as you relate with her words.

These pages started out as a woman with a dream. Then that woman was given the chance to step out in faith and dare to believe that God's desire in her heart would come to pass. She stepped into that place of learning, and as she did, God led her to know how He would download this assignment to her and the desire which He put into her heart long ago, through their very personal relationship with one another.

The way He does this is different for each person, as each person is made uniquely; He speaks differently to each as we are made in His image. God's special way of speaking to Susan has been explained to me as "dancing in my mind." I love this because the Holy Spirit literally has danced through Susan's mind giving choreographed images for every place the pure and blameless love of God shines through on these pages. Any woman can find herself in the dance, because we are all women just like the ones you're about to read about. You may be the star dancer or a background dancer, but I guarantee, you will find yourself somewhere in the dance with God leading.

As Susan took these dances and put them into words, she needed an intermission at times. Every great ballet or musical has part one, part two, and time for intermission! For Susan this intermission was a time to wrap up in a cozy quilt, as she herself is an expert quilt maker from Maine. Writing can be a daunting task, so she would pull out her favorite quilt and a nice cup of tea to relax before the next chapter began. So yes, you will read about the quilt squares. God invites you to do the same—grab your favorite quilt and a cup of tea, start to listen to the music of His heart and watch the dancers unfold Bible stories of women just like you, in a way you may never have seen or even dared to think of. Just know this: God has choreographed every word. Feel it in your spirit, let Him move you to healing.

Thank you, Susan, for your obedience to God's calling and the blessing of allowing us to be part of the Holy Spirit dance, *WOMEN JUST LIKE US*, while covered in the warmth of God's love.

Deborah Lovett
Author, Speaker and Writing Coach
www.deborahlovett.org
Author of *Gushing Springs*, *Arise out of the Ashes*, and *22 days in the County Jail*

# TUMBLING BLOCKS

## Genesis 3–4 ~ Eve

This quilt square is called *Tumbling Blocks*. From a distance it looks like the blocks are falling off the material. It reminds me of a woman in the Bible and of myself. Maybe you, too, can find yourself in this square.

For us, the tumbling starts with a small but simple reply to a request from a loved one or friend, "No, I can't," or "I'm sorry, I'm just not interested." Sometimes the reply starts with the truth, "I have too much to do," or even a half-hearted, "Yes, I can." The tumbling could start with something we say—occasionally without thinking, or by our words being misunderstood.

My favorite excuse is the one followed by second-guessing, "Why didn't I do that differently?" or "If only I had been more faithful, or disciplined my children more, or listened to and obeyed the Lord." I'm sure you get the picture and can fill in your own excuses.

The results are always the same, hurt, dejected looks, and the judgment of others; the silence that follows drag us down a path we've all taken at one time or another. What started out as small as a pebble soon morphs into a huge pile of rocks as we allow our minds to drift away from the Lord. One thought leads to another and soon we become overwhelmed, confused, defeated, and convinced that we are the worst person in the world. Sometimes, though, that judgment comes to us, not from ourselves, but from others.

While the Bible never really tells us how Eve felt or what she thought, I'm convinced that she, as a woman, had to feel some of the same emotions that we experience. Eve was the first woman, created by God Himself from Adam's rib, to be Adam's helpmeet and companion. She lived with Adam in a beautiful garden filled with trees, flowers, and animals. Her days were filled with joy and peace—no fighting, pain, or death as they did not exist. There was no real work to be done as the garden was perfect. One must wonder if she saw something new every day.

In the cool of the evening, she and Adam would walk in the garden and there they would fellowship with their God—their Creator. Did they talk to God about their day or the animals and their antics? Maybe they had discovered a new flower, insect, or bird. The most important part of that nightly routine was just being able to talk to God—to know they were loved by their Creator and could express their love to Him.

Then it happened. Eve was approached by the serpent while she was in the garden. He spoke to her, and she answered. It was Eve who believed what he said, and she was the one who offered the fruit to Adam. As they took a bite of that fruit, the world she knew changed; gone was her perfect home, perfect husband, her peace, and most important, her personal, perfect relationship with God. She heard her husband blame her for what had happened. With tears streaming down her face, she admitted to God what she had done. Then she and Adam heard that they could no longer live in the garden.

Can't you just picture her thinking, *if only I had not listened to the serpent and believed what he said; if only I hadn't picked the fruit and offered it to Adam*. It must have wrenched her heart as they took that final walk out of the garden. The skins of animals covered both her and her husband, and she knew that she had brought death into the world. I can almost hear her heart pleading as she whispered, "I want to start over please." As she turned teary-eyed for one last glimpse of the garden, she saw the guards God had placed there, barring their return—forever.

It wasn't long afterward a new and real world took over Eve's life. Every day there were meals to cook, a husband to feed and a house to clean. Soon the children started coming, Cain and Abel. Put yourself in Eve's place the first time one of her sons fell and got hurt, the first time she heard them argue and fight. They knew no other way, but Eve. . . she *did*.

She must have remembered the peace and tranquility of the garden where there was no work to be done, no pain, and no raised voices in anger to listen to. Then as the boys grew, they became so different from each other. Cain was the tiller of the land, daily struggling with weeds, thorns, insects, and the weather. Abel, on the other hand, was the keeper of the sheep, daily facing the struggles of life and death with his flock. Each night, Eve listened to her men as they discussed the trials of the day. She watched in grief as they flexed sore muscles and made plans for the next day. I wonder, as she turned her back to clean up after them, if she again pleaded for a re-do.

Since leaving the garden, death was so close; the plants, animals and crops all went through the cycle of life and death. The family learned to live with that cycle—until the day Cain killed Abel. I can just picture Eve, crumbling to the ground when she heard the news. Weeping, rocking back and forth, pleading with God, imploring Him to forgive her for the part she played, begging for the life she once knew, and asking for all the misery to stop. Thoughts came back as pictures played in her mind. Once again, she was in the garden, listening to the commands of God, but then disobeying Him—and the first pebble came. She saw the look on her husband's face as his eyes were opened to sin and destruction, with his first bite of the fruit—and another pebble was added—the animal skins, the guards at the entrance of the garden—another pebble piled on top. The struggle to make a living among thorns in a hostile land, occupied her mind and she placed still another pebble upon the pile. Although she knew it was all her fault, she never realized things would be this bad. If only she hadn't been so selfish, so curious. . . *if only*, and the pebbles came crashing down, leaving Eve in a sea of guilt and sorrow as she buried one son and watched God punish the other.

************************************************************************************************************

We've all been there. We make mistakes as women, as wives and as mothers. The men in our lives make similar mistakes. For some reason, though, our mistakes *seem to be* taken more to heart. Maybe it's because we come from Eve. There's a part of us that seems to feel the pain of our loved ones more deeply; their mistakes somehow become our fault, and we start playing the "if only" game. We fall into a pit of despair and depression, worried about what other people think of us and our families. Soon we're spiraling downward, analyzing every inadequacy, piling pebbles into blocks of failure**,** and *into* a wall, until it shuts out the voice of our Beloved Father. The wall convinces us that like Eve, we are bad wives and mothers. We are failures.

Like Eve, we have sinned and yes, our sins affect others. We may not have done everything right, but nobody else has either. As women, we need to let the wall of guilt, blame and judgment that we have built (or that others have created with their judgments), come tumbling down. We do not have to live a life of condemnation.

Before Eve left the garden, God promised there would be a Savior who would take away the sins of the world. Eve never saw the fulfillment of that promise, but we have. John 3:16 says,

"For God so loved the world, that he gave his only begotten Son, that whosoever believeth in him should not perish, but have everlasting life" (KJV).

As daughters of the King, we need to stop believing the deceiver and his lies. Instead, we need to start believing the Lord who loves us so much that He sent His Son to the cross to die in our place. He is waiting for us to come to Him, to accept His offer of love and forgiveness of sin; if you've never done that before, do it today. If you *have* accepted Jesus as your Savior and Lord already, confess to Him the lies you have been believing, and read and claim His Word for your life.

*********************************************************************************************************

- What lies are you believing today?

- Are you hiding behind a wall? What is it made of?

- What would change in your life if you let the walls down?

- Have you ever asked Jesus Christ to be your Savior?

- Have you ever made Him Lord of your life?

Loss
Attitudes
Safety
Fear
Home
Friends
Decisions
TRUST
Questions
Known
Family
unknown

# SUITCASE

## Genesis 6:14-9:18 ~ Mrs. Noah

I have it all packed—one basket with clothes for me and my husband. I am not sure of where this trip will lead or what I will find at the end of it. I just know that we have been chosen to travel it. I hate to leave this place; it is all that I know. It was here that I came on the day of my wedding and have stayed ever since. This is my home where my boys grew up and got married— where all my friends and memories are—yet today all this changes. It isn't as if the trip has come by surprise; one would have thought that after 120 years, I would be better prepared.

So many things have happened in the years we've been here. You see, my husband Noah, was called by God to build an ark. The fact that Noah was asked to build an ark didn't seem as strange as the next piece of news; Noah also told us that God said it is going to rain. We have no idea what rain is. The ground is watered from below; nothing has ever fallen from the sky. But Noah was not done—not only was it going to rain, but there would also be a flood and anyone not in the ark would die. God had gone on to tell him how big to make the ark and how much food and water to take on it for us and the animals. Well, at least I understood that part; our family and our animals were coming with us. Noah continued and said that there would be two of every unclean animal and seven of every clean one. At that point, I was ready to say, "No!" Wild animals? Wild animals with my family trapped on an ark while it did something called rain—THAT I was not sure of. Noah reminded me that the God whom we follow had called Him and we were to be faithful.

My front yard was turned into a lumber yard, filled with trees, boards and men calling out measurements. The sound of hammers and saws filled our days. Noah tried to tell the men what was going to happen, but they just laughed at him. Noah came home every night excited on one hand about the progress but saddened by the disbelief in his workers. I had tried to talk to our family and friends about what Noah was building and why, but they only called him crazy. It broke my heart when my family and friends from childhood laughed at me and talked behind my back. They thought we were nuts.

The ark had been finished only a little while when there was a loud rumbling coming from all directions. The ground shook under our feet. Before I could figure out what was going on, the sky above me turned black and the sound of wings beating drowned out any conversation. I stood with my daughters-in-law in the doorway of our home and watched as wild animals of all sorts walked slowly and orderly into the ark. Mortal enemies stood one behind the other waiting in line to climb up the gangplank and be led to a stall by one of my sons. I looked around and all our friends and family were standing with their mouths open, watching. This I thought would help them believe, so I went to share with them once again. This time I had proof; the animals had come just as God had said. The rain would be next and then the flood. I pleaded, begged, and cried, to no avail; they shook their heads and walked away.

Our sons and their wives entered the ark with a final plea for their families to join them going unheeded. In tears, they disappeared into the darkness of the ark. Then it was our turn. I looked around and locked my arm into Noah's as we walked up the gangplank. Before we entered, we gave one more desperate plea for our family and friends to believe and join us. Instead, their laughter and words of scorn and disbelief were thrown back at us. Noah leaned down and whispered it was time; with tears running down my face, we entered our new home. The sound of the door closing behind us sealed not only our fate but that of those on the other side as well.

We sat in silence waiting, but for what exactly we did not know. Even the animals were eerily quiet. Then we heard it—something hitting the outside of the ark. After a while, we began to feel a motion like we were rocking. Then in the distance we could hear the call of those we had to leave behind. With fear in their voices, they were yelling and asking to come aboard; they said they believed and were sorry. I would have gladly let them come aboard, but the door had no handle on my side; I could not open it. Their fate was sealed and there was nothing I could do to help. I sat with my head in my hands and cried. I begged God to change His plan—to stop the rain, as these were people I loved; they were my family and friends—there were older people along with children and babies. My heart broke into pieces. I have never felt more helpless or hopeless in all my life. There was nothing I could do; it was not something I could fix.

Soon the rocking intensified and the sound of the waves hitting the outside of the ark matched the rhythm of what had to be the rain hitting the roof. My new life had begun. For the next 370 days my life consisted of my husband, 3 sons and their wives, animals, and no view of the outside world. As women, we did the cooking, tried to keep the living areas clean, did laundry and talked about what we thought it was going to be like when we got out of the ark. When my ark companions became too much for me, I wandered among the animals, spending time talking to them and petting them. By the time the ark bumped to a stop, everyone was getting a little bit stressed.

Finally, we were able to open a small window. I was so excited when Noah let the dove out, but we were all heartbroken when it came back. Seven days later, Noah released the dove again and it came back with an olive leaf in its beak—a third time and the dove never returned. At last, the door to the ark opened and the animals went out two by two just as quietly and orderly as they had come in. The birds flew off with their songs filling the air. The boys and their wives along with Noah and I stood on the gangplank looking around. Nothing looked familiar; no one that we loved was left. We were in a new world—just the eight of us. Sorrow, fear, and excitement filled my heart all at the same time; a new beginning was being offered—yet I desired the safe old world I once knew. Once again, I realized I was on a journey I had not asked for. Putting my hand into Noah's, I walked down the gangplank and into my new normal.

***************************************************************************************************

- Have you ever had to get use to a new normal?

- Describe what brought it to pass?

- How has it changed you? Your family?

- Did it shake or grow your faith?

***************************************************************************************************

Mrs. Noah's quilt square is a suitcase. Her case was filled with what she expected to need as she followed the leading of her God. Little did she know, it wasn't what was in the suitcase that she really needed. The suitcase reminds me that we can prepare for changes and challenges of life, but in reality, it's what's in our heart that truly allows us to follow the Lord.

Life has a way of going along safe and normal and we think because we are believers, we will be okay; bad things happen to other people but not to us. . . until that day when the road falls out from under our feet—the phone rings, the email or text comes, you get called into the boss's office, or the doctor says, "I'm sorry to tell you this, but…" Maybe it comes with a knock on the door, fire trucks in your yard, or standing beside the grave of a loved one. Sooner or later, we all like Mrs. Noah will find ourselves on a road that we did not choose or want to travel but must—a road we cannot get off and one we must travel to the end. There is only one way to travel this road and that is to follow Mrs. Noah's example: hang on to your faith and take the hand of the One who has set you on that road in the first place—the One who will never leave you or forsake you.

Press your ear as close to the Lord's heart as you can and listen to His heartbeat till all the voices and sounds of the storm raging outside are silenced. Let Him carry you through the attacks, doubts, and heart wrenching moments filled with tears, till the end. While we will emerge changed forever, we will also have a deeper belief and trust in the One who is still holding our hand as we step into our new normal. Jeremiah 29:11 says, "For I know the thoughts that I think toward you, saith the LORD, thoughts of peace, and not of evil, to give you an expected end" (KJV).

# 3

# HOPE

Exodus 2:1-10, 6:10 ~ Jochebed


Jochebed knew time was running out. The little one sleeping peacefully in her arms had gotten so big, it was harder each day to keep him hidden.  Her mind went back to the day she realized she was expecting again. It should have been a time of rejoicing and laughter for our family as Jehovah rained His blessing down on us once more; He was showing the world that I was blessed by Him. While her head knew this, her heart was breaking as the questions, "But why now?" and "What if?" raced through her thoughts each day. She would be doing routine tasks when fear would unexpectedly whelm up in her soul and overtake her.

For many months, Jochebed wept and silently pleaded with Jehovah to make this new child a girl. Their daughter, Miriam, was a sweet blessing, joyfully breaking out in song at the least little thing. *She certainly brightened our dark days, and a baby girl would be safe*, Jochebed thought. Aaron, their eldest, was a loving, helpful, solemn little man. *Aaron will carry on the line of Levi and make us proud.*

But when her midwife told her she had a son, Jochebed's heart was crushed. Could her faith survive if this dear little boy, like all newborn Israelite male babies, was seized and drowned in the Nile? What would she tell Miriam and Aaron when their little brother was thrown into the river? Jochebed wondered if she herself would become another of those mothers who walked the streets outside with vacant stares, empty arms and tear-filled eyes.

She lifted her face to the heavens and pondered, *where are you, great Jehovah? Why aren't You helping us? Aren't we Israelites Your chosen people? Didn't You lead us here in the time of Joseph to preserve us?* Yet now, it seemed death walked through His people weekly, since the decree that every boy born to the Hebrews was sentenced to death—all because the new Pharaoh of Egypt was afraid of the Hebrew people. It was true their number had grown from the time of Joseph, yet they were peaceful people. They were chosen by God Almighty—His people yet now the heavens were silent. There was no help to be found and innocent little boys were dying. Where was their God when they clearly needed Him?

She was brought back to the present by a commotion outside. She heard the footsteps of rushing soldiers, the crying of a newborn, the pleading of his father and screams of agony from his mother. Jochebed hugged Moses closer as tears ran down her face. He moved in her arms; the wailing grief outside had caused him to wake up crying. She quickly nursed him to calm him and held him a little tighter as the tears ran down her face. She recognized the voices of the parents, who like she and so many others, had been praying for a daughter—but instead, produced a son. *Where was Jehovah? All He had to do was move and all this would stop.* They had been praying, confessing their sins and offering the sacrifices, but He had not yet caused anything to change.

Jochebed had no need to remind herself that he was very much alive and nestled in her arms as the warmth of his little body against hers blessed her heart. She glanced down at his face; his long eye lashes moved as he slept and a grimace or maybe a smile danced on his lips. *The second I laid eyes on you, I knew there was something special about you*. She hadn't been the only one to recognize it; his father had seen it as well. At once, they would do whatever was necessary to protect him. The first days, they did not celebrate his birth; they made sure the older children said nothing about him to anyone. It had been easy those first two months, to hide herself and the baby in their home. But now, he had changed and discovered his voice; they could no longer shield him. *Where? Where are you, Jehovah? All You need to do is move. You could stop this at any time. What are You waiting for? Where are You? We've all been praying, confessing our sins—and yet, You are silent; Your children are dying.*

It was Jochebed's husband who had come up with the idea of the basket made of bulrushes. During the day, Miriam and Aaron gathered them from the edges of the Nile. Each evening, the family worked on the basket while the baby slept. Aaron and Miriam listened silently as their father told them how Jehovah had saved His people throughout the ages, but Jochebed hid her tears as she wept and quietly questioned Jehovah again. *Are You going to save us? Or have You forgotten us?*

Suddenly it seemed, the morning they had all dreaded arrived.  Her husband walked over and lifted their infant son from his bed. She could hear him murmuring a blessing over Moses before placing him in her arms and leaving the room. Jochebed held her baby closer, knowing this was the last time she would ever hold him. With her finger, she traced every contour of his face, bending forward to kiss his little head. She told him about their great God, Jehovah, and the mighty things He had done. She whispered his name, "Moses" when he opened his eyes and smiled at her, but she felt as if her heart were being ripped right out of her body. Miriam sat at her feet and watched everything quietly, somehow aware that this was different, that it was a special time between a mother and her son.

It wasn't much later that Jochebed's husband and older son came into the room. Aaron walked solemnly to the bed and with tears in his eyes, leaned down to kiss his brother goodbye. He turned away quickly and went to his father's side, and they left together sobbing.

Jochebed knew it was time. Rising, she changed the baby's diaper, dressed him and called for Miriam. After they had all kissed Moses and reminded him, he was loved, they placed him in the basket. Their grief was unbearable and there was no stopping the tears that flowed down their faces as they walked to the edge of the river. Jochebed knelt one last time and lifted the cover of the basket. She was thankful he was sleeping and didn't know what was about to happen.

Slowly she placed the basket in the water and gave it a gentle push. When it was out of reach, she turned and headed home. Her heart was torn with anguish, her spirit was crushed by questions. *What kind of mother does this to her child? Was it better to be the one who put him in the river, instead of common vulgar soldiers? Would Jehovah watch over him? Was Moses as special as they had thought? Would he feel pain if he were to drown?*

She wanted to rescue him, to save him, but knew she couldn't. The minute she let go of the basket, she lost control of him; now she had to trust—to trust Jehovah—the One who *seemed* so distant and detached. There was nothing more she could do. As she entered her house and sat down, she began to cry, unable to stop as she waited for a yet-unknown result. Never in her life had she felt so helpless and alone! Yet she knew she had to trust Jehovah regardless of what her heart was feeling.

Her crying was interrupted by Miriam, racing through the door calling to her. As Miriam caught her breath, she explained, "The princess has found Moses and declared she would raise him as her own!" The princess, however, needed a nurse maid for him and Miriam had hurried home to get her mother.

Jochebed rushed off. Bowing before the princess, she listened to how she was to take this baby boy home and raise him until he was weaned, then return him. Jochebed ached to grab her son but instead, calmly and gently took him and walked away. She knew someday, she would have to give him up again, but by then he would know about Jehovah. Moses would also know how his family had saved him from certain death. She would tell him Jehovah God was faithful, even when it *seemed* He wasn't. That night, there was great rejoicing and celebration in their home; once more, Jehovah had answered their prayers.

****************************************************************************************************

Ever been there? You know that spot in your life where you have searched for God and pled with Him, asked Him the questions that pressed in your heart, but received no answer? The time you had to let go and put your most precious dream, child, job, home, or loved one into the hands of God—and walk away? You knew you had searched the heavens, prayed till you had no words left, asked others to pray, and still there was only silence. There was nothing more to be done; someone else would decide the outcome and you just had to sit back and watch it happen—and sometimes, it was like watching a bad movie. Your heart questioned, *Is He still God? Does He still care? Is He still in control? Why doesn't He act?* Yet like Jochebed, you had a place deep inside you that *knew* the answer to all those questions was, *yes*.

- What verse do you cling to in those times?

- Is there a place or time you can *REVISIT* that proves He has met your needs before?

- What if you do not get the same answer Jochebed did? Will you in your disappointment still believe?

****************************************************************************************************

I am positive Jochebed questioned God, herself and her faith. Yet through it all, she knew that she *knew,* He was totally faithful and loving and was going to deliver them once again, for her God never broke His promises. You, my friend, can stand on those same promises. God *is* faithful and loving and has a plan even when we can't see it—or understand His ways.

I'm not sure if Jochebed was one of the people Moses led to the promised land, yet I *am* sure there were those in that number who had heard the story of his mother's *faith* and God's provision.

Just like Moses, we will always be used to glorify God. Therefore, Jochebed's quilt square must be one named Hope; the shades of dark and light remind us that even in the darkest times there is always the hope that faith in Christ can give. We may not always get the answer we want but we still need to believe; when it seems there is nothing else left, we can still choose to hope in the One who loves us and has a plan for us.

# 4

# Open Heart

## 1 Samuel 1 ~ Hannah

Prayer: talking to God, placing our requests before His throne daily. Easy enough for a child to learn and it's what most of us do every day.

Yet the prayer that changes who you are is the prayer that rips at your heart and breaks *it* in two—the one that takes you to your knees, face on the floor, tears pooling around you and the prayer that makes you promise anything, if only God would answer. These times of prayer *are* between you and your God. Friends may care, but only HE can understand the anguish you are going through. These prayers are a battle of life and death, sometimes literally but always emotionally. You go one on one with God—and the battle doesn't end until you have an answer. During this time, you do not care what people think or how long it takes because this is personal; your faith and life depend on it.

That had to be how it was with Hannah; she'd had enough. It didn't matter that her husband loved her more than his other wife. Neither did it matter that he offered her twice as much as he gave Peninnah, who after all, had borne all his children. She snipped at Hannah constantly. Peninnah's children meant God had blessed her, whereas in the sight of others, Hannah's barrenness meant God had closed her womb because she did not please Him. On top of that, it was time to go to Shiloh to offer the yearly sacrifice to their God. It is no wonder Hannah refused to eat and only cried; the loneliness in her arms, combined with constant gloating comments from Peninnah, drove Hannah to the Lord.

No longer could she contain herself. Abruptly, she rose and leaving their temporary home, ran toward the temple. As she gathered speed, she could hear her husband calling her name, while Peninnah undoubtedly claimed innocence in the whole matter. Hannah's tears fell freely and at times clouded the trail in front of her. She had listened long enough to well-wishers and those who accused. No one, not even her husband could solve this situation.

As she ran, Hannah resolved in her mind that she would go to the source, to her God and plead her case. Her dress whipped wildly around her legs, almost falling as she stepped into the empty temple. She was at the end of herself; she had nothing left to offer except tears and as they fell freely, she dropped to her knees, her face to the floor. There she poured out her pain and anguish before her God. There were no words spoken as a broken heart has no real words; Hannah's mouth moved as God listened to her heart. There, in the house of God, she made a vow before the Lord. If He would bless her with a son, she would give him back to serve the Lord all the days of his life as soon as he was weaned. While she was pleading before God, Eli the high priest watched and thought she was drunk.

"How long wilt thou be drunken? Put away thy wine from thee,"[1] he said to her. Hannah answered him right away, assuring him that she was not drunk but in fact a woman with a very sorrowful heart. She continued to assure Eli that she had just been pouring out her soul before

---

[1] 1 Samuel 1:14 KJV

her God, so Eli confirmed to Hannah that she could go in peace, that God had heard her plea and had answered.

No one can be the same after that kind of season of deep prayer; it changes the very core of who you are. The Hannah who abruptly left her family earlier that day was not the same Hannah who came back. She would never be the same again. Her faith in her God was unshakeable; she stood taller, was confident, and at peace. She had pleaded her case before God, and He had heard and answered.

The family returned home and to the normal activities of cooking, cleaning and caring for children. As each day passed Hannah waited patiently for her answer. The jabs from Peninnah didn't bring the same reaction they once had. Instead of weeping, Hannah was more content and smiled as if she knew something the rest of the world didn't.

Then one day it happened—the first flutter! Hannah stopped in the middle of her chores and put her hand over her belly. She raised her face to the heavens as tears of joy fell freely from her eyes, and her lips moved, once again wordlessly. She would sing praises to her God for His faithfulness in her life. There wasn't a day in those months of waiting when Hannah wasn't found telling someone how God had heard and answered her prayers. Those who believed in her God joined her in praise while others shook their heads in unbelief.

Then it was time. The pains of birth racked her body and soon, a son was wrapped and placed in her arms. Hannah counted his fingers and toes—touched the dark hair on his head. It was surreal; she was holding a baby. . . but this was no ordinary baby—it was HER baby she held in her arms. She was FINALLY a mother. God had blessed her and all those who were close by heard her words of praise and thanksgiving.

As little Samuel slept after his feeding that night, Hannah told him for the first time how he was an answer to prayer. It would be a story that would be retold to him for the rest of his life.

When it came time to go to Shiloh the next year, Hannah stayed behind and she would not go again until it was time to fulfill her promise to God and little Samuel was weaned.

In Hannah's eyes, time never moved so fast, as he went from crying at night to crawling to walking and talking. She took every possible opportunity that she could to tell him about their God. From the miracles in the times of Noah and Moses, to the miracle of his birth. She had never seen color so bright or laughed so deep as she did with him. But too soon it seemed, he was weaned, *and* now at the young age of five, it was time.

She packed his bag, including the clothes she had stitched at night while watching him sleep. Clothes that were far too big for him now, but he would grow into in the following months—when she would not be there. As she slipped into his room the night before the trip, she noticed that he looked so small, and there was so much more she wanted to teach him. As she felt her heart break, she settled down next to him. His small body curled into her arms as new tears fell. Hannah knew that tomorrow she and little Samuel would return to Shiloh with their family, and they would never be the same again.

Hannah watched her son play with his brothers and sisters as they traveled. He was so young, so innocent and vulnerable. Had she taught him everything he would need to know? Would he remember how much she loved him? Even though she knew what she had to do, even though she believed that God was in control, she was still a mother and Samuel was still her son. So, with her heart breaking, Hannah slipped away from her family once again returning, like we all do eventually, to the temple—the very same place where she battled inprayer.

This time the battle was different. This was no longer an issue of want; this time it was an issue of obedience. Once more, Hannah found herself on her knees, tears streaming down her face, her lips moving without a sound as grief crushed her heart before the throne of her God.

She begged for any other way to fulfill the promise she had made. The idea of leaving her small son there was more than she could take.

The man who would raise her son was the same one who had accused her of being drunk; the same man whose sons were not following God. There had to be another way. Yet the battle was finally won when Hannah remembered how faithful God had been in the past. She raised her face and praised God, thanked Him for His gift of her son, wiped her tears and walked with him back to her family.

The next morning the family followed Hannah as she led Samuel by the hand to the temple. They gave Samuel kisses and hugs, then stepped back to give Hannah some time alone with him. They watched as Hannah knelt before him to tell him one more time about him being an answer to prayer. She reminded him that he was being given back to God to serve Him in the temple.

She promised to return every year; she gave him a kiss and drew his small body in for a long hug. She whispered her love for him in his ear. Then standing up she turned and walked away, so he would not see her weeping. As she walked home, she began counting the days till she could once again hold him in her arms.

Just as those of us who have battled on our knees, our hearts breaking before the throne of our God, Hannah was forever changed from her battle. She knew in her very core that her God loved her and had strengthened her. She could bring anything before his throne because He would hear and answer her.

********************************************************************************************************

- Have you ever battled in prayer like Hannah?

- What was the pain that was so deep that there were no words to express your grief?

- Did you find Him faithful?

- How has your relationship with the Lord changed because of that battle?

*******************************************************************************************************

Hannah's quilt square is the open heart. Everything she desired and loved she gave to her Lord without withholding anything. With that surrender came peace and the ability to live the rest of her life trusting Him.

Like some of you, too I have been on that battlefield. There is no way I will ever forget those moments. When my world crashed down on me, I had no words to explain the agony and heartbreak I was feeling. There was no one on this earth who could understand my pain, even if he or she had experienced the same losses. Why? Because for each of us, it is personal, and we respond differently. Our heart-needs are different. Since God has created us with His own hands, He alone is the One who understands His reasons, even when we do not. It's because of those times of prayer I realize how much my Heavenly Father loves me, hears me and holds me close in His arms. I've opened my heart to the only One who can heal me. And He has.

Psalms 147:3-5 says, "He healeth the broken in heart, and bindeth up their wounds. He telleth the number of the stars; he calleth them all by their names. Great is our Lord, and of great power: his understanding is infinite" (KJV).

# 5

# Job's Troubles

## Job 1-2, 42:12-13 ~ Job's Wife

You know, a lot of things in life are not fair. First, for example, I am given no name in the Bible. It is as if I really don't matter in the whole scheme of things, or I was not important. Second, just because of one little sentence I uttered—probably without realizing it would be recorded for eternity—I was branded a terrible woman. Yet please indulge me if I could possibly take some of your time. I'd like to tell you the rest of my story.

I was born and raised in a culture that did not value women. Oh, we had our place and our jobs. Our place was in the home, and our jobs were cooking, cleaning, sewing, birthing children and honoring our husbands. We were also called upon to carry water for our homes and the animals, to tend our gardens and shop. My day would begin before the sun rose in the east and it would not end till the last candle went out at night, and I would be the one putting it out. Mind you, I am not complaining one single bit. There were benefits to this lifestyle—one of them being, I never worried about my weight. On a more serious note, I knew that my husband and I had been blessed by our God, Jehovah. I had given birth and raised seven handsome and strong sons and three beautiful daughters. Granted they were not perfect, but they were our pride and joy. In all the years since I said, "I do" to my husband, I worked beside him to help him in everything he did. In the words of the Bible (not my words, mind you), he was "the greatest of all men of the east." Yes, you guessed it, Job was my husband and I, his nameless wife.

If you know the story, in one day, just one twenty-four-hour period, everything we had was gone. First, the Sabenas took our oxen and asses. Next, fire took all our sheep and servants; together that was eight thousand and five hundred animals, then unnumbered servants.

I thought the day could not get any worse. I was on my way to comfort my husband when I heard that our three thousand camels had been captured as well. We had no flocks or herds left but we still had each other and our children. I knew that we could, with Jehovah's help, build it all back up again. Even though my heart was breaking with the loss of life, I knew that we could buy more animals and hire more servants.

Nothing could have prepared me for the next piece of news that reached my ears. Our children, all ten of them were dead, crushed when the house fell in as they were eating together. My mind couldn't take any more; I was devastated and crushed beyond words. Put yourself in my place—first, the family business, which I could take, but my children? My babies? All ten of them were gone! I knew I would never see them again on this earth; I absolutely wanted to die. Job though stayed strong through all of this; he reminded me that we came into the world with nothing and would leave the same way. Personally, I was ready to leave this world right then.

It wasn't but a few days later Job came down with this awful condition—boils. It made him itch, so he took a piece of pottery and scraped his skin with it. As if boils were not bad enough, he went and sat down on a pile of ashes. Well, if you know the story, you know that was when I made my famous one liner, "Dost thou still retain thine integrity? Curse God and die."[2]

Please try to understand, I was taught that if there was sin in someone's life, Jehovah dealt with him. I just needed to know if Job still thought he was blameless. In my pain and anger I thought that maybe there was some sin in his life that he needed to confess. My heart was also involved in that question; I watched the man I love suffer. My heart was breaking for him, for not only had he lost his children as well as I, but he had lost his standing in the community. All those emotions combined led to that one statement. You see, I wasn't given the privilege to know what you already know—that this all happened with God's permission, to test, if you will, Job's faith. I made that comment out of pain; I had lost everything as well, including my children. My children showed people that Jehovah had blessed me—that I, too, had standing. My sons were supposed to take care of me when I was older if Job died first. I had nothing left in this world. I felt as though God Himself had turned against Job—and against me.

No, I agree. There is no excuse for what I said; my faith was not that strong. I will admit that. But I only saw the here and now. Remember, I am a woman with all the emotions that you have. I didn't mean for it to sound so harsh, so unloving, so unbelieving; it was my *pain* speaking. My sorrow was so great and deep that it overshadowed my faith in my God; yet I never completely lost my trust in my Creator.

********************************************************************************************

- Before today, did you ever stop to think about Job's wife and her feelings?

- Have you ever been to the place where your grief is stronger than your faith?

---

[2] Job 2:9 KJV

Maybe you, like me, have stood judged and condemned by peers and others without being able to give your side of the story. The judgment has been passed and we are forever labeled, Faithless, Liar, Untrustworthy, Gossip, a Bad Parent, Unfaithful, and Unworthy, just to name a few. The labels only add to the pain and loneliness that we are feeling. I've been there, and I'm sure if you are honest, you have too. Then again, I have also been the one who judged others and put those labels on them, never once thinking about what they were going through.

- Can you think of a time that you were judged and labeled?

- How did it make you feel? Think of strong adjectives to illustrate this.

- Do those words still hurt?

- Have you forgiven the person or people who judged you?

We think as we pass judgment on others, that we know the whole story based on hearsay, but we do not. In reality, until each of us takes the time to really listen to the grieving with our heart and not our mind, we cannot know or understand. Until we are willing—even for a few minutes—to climb into their place and try to comprehend what the other person is going through, we have no real right to pass judgment. Even after hearing the whole story, we still need to be careful not to pass judgment on others.

Matthew 7:1-3 says, "Do not judge, or you too will be judged. For in the same way you judge others, you will be judged, and with the measure you use, it will be measured to you. "Why do you look at the speck of sawdust in your brother's eye and pay no attention to the plank in your own eye" (NIV)?

*******************************************************************************************************

Job's wife is never heard of again in that book until the very end. Though many condemned her for her words, God blessed her in a way that all could see. He gave her seven more sons and three more daughters.

The quilt square that represents Job's wife is called *Job's Troubles*; it looks like points on a compass. The points signify, that troubles came upon Job from all directions. I would like to add that the name probably should be *Mr. and Mrs. Job's Troubles*, for she went through everything he did.

By the way, the next time you hear Job's story and people start remarking about his wife, please remind them that she was just a woman with a broken heart. Please also remember that each person you meet has a story that you do not know. The words you speak may have the power to heal or break someone; speak prayerfully for you never know what trial they are facing.

# 6

# ALL POINTS IN

## Luke 10 ~ Martha

In her mind, she was five again, standing in the familiar cooking area of her family's home. Her mother was teaching her about her role in the world. It was almost as if she could hear her sweet voice again after many long years, "Your job is to keep the house clean and cook the meals. Every need your family has will be your job. That is why you must learn to cook and clean now instead of playing." She smiled to herself as she reached for more flour, remembering the cooking lessons that started that very day and continued for years to come.

Yes, every job in *this* house appeared to be hers and hers alone. Most days it didn't bother her to wake up before dawn, get dressed and start the fire, light the candles and get water from the well. When the family woke up, the food was almost ready. Yet this wasn't the family her mother had spoken of. Once again, her mind went back to the old familiar cooking area and the words of her mother, "Someday, a young man will ask for your hand in marriage, and then you will move away and start your own family. You will need to know not only how to cook and clean, but how to sew clothing, take care of little ones and manage money." Martha kneaded the bread and smiled sadly. There had been no young man asking for her hand—at least, not yet.

*I'm getting older by the day,* she thought as she absentmindedly brushed some hair out of her eyes with flour-covered hands. In reality, she did have a family of sorts and she was responsible for them. Martha sighed deeply. *I'll probably never experience the joy my parents had, of welcoming a new baby into my family.*

Once again, her mind floated back, but this time, to the day her brother was born. The family was so excited God had given them a son. There would be someone to carry on the family name, they said. This had caused her child-sized heart to be troubled, *was her name not the same as this squalling baby?* Martha had wiggled her finger and her father came down to her level to hear what she had to say; she spoke earnestly of her concern about the family name. "It has to be a son to carry on the family name," he explained. "You, my daughter, will marry and your name will change." He patted her head, smiling.

She shook her head and laughed as she remembered the hurt feelings she had carried around for months. Martha had almost hated her brother because he could always have the family name. Now she laughed out loud, wishing that she'd had her name changed and wasn't still carrying her father's name at her age. She heard the door open and turned as her younger sister came running into the kitchen looking for her.

"He's here! He's here, and He is coming to spend some time with us. I've invited Him to eat with us today. I can't wait! Aren't you excited? This will be so much fun. I must go tell everyone." Her little sister rushed in and out so fast, that Martha couldn't even think to speak. Company coming! She looked quickly around. The house was a mess—and then there was food to be prepared. *So much to do! Where do I start?* she thought as she rushed to catch Mary before she left, but the door was already closed and her sister was gone, running down the road.

As she stood in the doorway she announced to an empty room, "Isn't that just like my sister. Mary has been that way since birth. Always in a hurry, never having the time to learn the things she was supposed to. No time for cooking lessons, and when she needs to cook. . . watch out. Our parents tried to tame her before they died, just as I have since, but there's been little improvement."

Flustered, Martha picked up a dust rag and started to straighten the room up, while in her mind she began planning the menu and figuring out just how much time she had before the company arrived. Would He be alone, or would there be others with Him? A full course meal would be needed—of course, anything less would be an insult to the Teacher. She sighed and headed to the cooking area once again.

It seemed as if she had been on her feet for hours, and actually. . . she had.  Martha tried to ignore the conversation that was going on in the other room. The company had come. Her brother of course, sat down to talk and listen to the Teacher; that was expected, yet Mary, her little sister, had also sat down, not caring that Martha was doing all the work.

With every exclamation and laugh, Martha grew angrier and angrier. It wasn't fair! When would *she* be able to sit down and listen? They didn't have this kind of company every day; who knew when He would come back**?** Then like a slap in the face, Martha heard Mary talking to Him. They had completely forgotten about her, as if she were nothing more than a servant.

*Enough!* she thought. *I've been working all day by myself and there's still more work to be done. My sister needs to be here helping me, and if my brother won't make her, I know who will.* Throwing down her apron upon the floor and dusting off her hands, she bolted into the room where the company sat. She didn't notice the looks of surprise as she interrupted the conversation. She didn't really care, but things would be fair now. She announced loudly, "Lord, dost thou not care that my sister hath left me to serve alone? Bid her therefore that she help me."[3] There was a hush in the room. All eyes turned from her to the Lord as He said, "Martha, Martha, thou art careful and troubled about many things: but one thing is needed: and Mary hath chosen that good part, which shall not be taken from her."[4]

Martha hurried back into the kitchen, sat down, and wept into her apron. She thought she was doing exactly what she was supposed to do—what she had been trained to do. Her shame at His gentle rebuke broke her heart. She sat there alone with tears streaming down her face, wondering where she had gone so wrong.

*****************************************************************************************************

- Have there been times when you tried your best and yet felt like a failure?

- Have you ever been jealous of someone?

- How do you handle those feelings?

- Do you let things build up until you blow up?

Martha's quilt square is called *All Points Inward*. Like the quilt square, Martha looked great from a distance. She seemed to always be taking care of others and having their best interests at heart. She kept doing what was expected of her and yet in reality, her heart told a different story through her actions.

Any quilt maker will tell you that even though her quilt looks beautiful and perfect, there are mistakes and she, as its creator, knows where each one is. I think as women, we all try to do our best. We work hard to prove our value, whether at home, a job or even in our churches.

---

[3] Luke 10:40 KJV
[4] Luke 10:41 KJV

We compare ourselves to others and fret when it seems they aren't pulling their own weight. Then, we start to become bitter and tell ourselves stories that aren't really true. Our stories become our truth and like Martha, we worry about many things that are not important.

I sincerely believe Martha truly loved Jesus and wanted to serve Him with the best that she had, with the gifts that she had been given. Unfortunately, her eyes strayed from Jesus, and she started to concentrate on everything else going on. Martha became conformed to this world; she lost the reason for her service. May we as women remember who our eyes should be focused on. We are not to compare ourselves with others or even watch what they are doing. We are not to keep score. The One whom we are supposed to be serving first and foremost, *is* our Lord and Savior. If we keep Him uppermost in our minds, everything else will fall into place. Romans 12:2 says, "And be not conformed to this world: but be ye transformed by the renewing of your mind, that ye may prove what is that good, and acceptable, and perfect, will of God" (KJV).

Like the quilt that looks perfect, we often lead others to believe that we are perfect, however, our Creator knows differently; we have all sinned and come short of the glory of God. No matter how much Martha served, or you and I do, we cannot earn our way into heaven. All of Martha's works and ours are as filthy rags in God's eyes. We were born sinners, yet while we were sinners, Jesus came to earth as a baby, grew up and was nailed to a cross. While He hung on that cross, He paid for every single sin that we have ever done or will ever do. No matter how much we do the right thing we can never earn our way into heaven. Jesus paid it all.

# 7

# Log Cabin Heart

## John 11 ~ Mary of Bethany

I am Mary of Bethany, the sister of Lazarus and Martha. I am sure that you have heard everything about me from my sister Martha. Yes, I did run into the house to tell her that Jesus was coming to visit. I also ran back out and left her to prepare the house as well as all the food. It isn't that I didn't know how to do the household chores, there are just other things that are more important in life. Martha was not happy with me as I sat at the feet of Jesus that day; honestly, I just wasn't thinking of anything but listening to what Jesus had to say. His words touched my heart and there was this deep longing of my soul to hear more. I wanted to hear every word that He said, so I forgot that there was anyone else in the room or that I had responsibilities.

Unfortunately, though, I certainly heard how Martha felt about me that day. She was right you know. I should have been helping her. That was my position as a woman; only the men were to sit around and listen to the teacher. I almost got up to help Martha, I was so embarrassed, yet the words of Jesus stopped me. He said that I had chosen the better thing and it would not be taken away from me. Martha quietly went back to the kitchen, and I continued to sit at the feet of Jesus and wondered what He meant that I had chosen the better thing. Sometimes I do not understand this teacher, but I have to admit, my heart and soul is drawn to Him.

After Jesus left that day, Martha and I talked about what happened; Martha seemed to have been changed by the words of Jesus. We apologized to each other and then went on with our lives. Then later, our whole world changed in an instant; Lazarus was sick. This was not a normal, temporary sickness. We knew that this sickness would take our brother away. There was only one thing to do. . . send for Jesus. So, we sent a messenger to go to Him and tell Him that the one He loved was sick.

As we waited for Jesus to come, we took turns taking care of Lazarus. Martha and I knew Jesus loved us and would not let us down. But sadly, the worst possible thing that could happen, happened. Lazarus died. Martha and I were heartbroken; Jesus had not come in time. We prepared the body and buried our brother the same day. Afterward, we just sat together, each of us lost in our own thoughts. . . *Why hadn't Jesus come? He was only a day's journey away.*

My heart was crushed. I didn't understand and I had so many questions; the biggest was, *didn't He love us?* Secondly, *if He did love us, why did Lazarus die? Who would take care of us now?* It wasn't like we could get a job. With no father, husband, or brother to take care of us, we would become a burden to the next male relative. *What if Martha and I couldn't go to the same house? Could I live without my sister AND my brother?* I don't think I could bear to lose Martha too.

It was four days *after* we buried Lazarus that Jesus finally came into town. Our friends could not wait to tell us that He was coming. Unlike the other times, it was Martha who ran to meet Him; I stayed behind, and just sat in the house. Martha had changed since Jesus had corrected her that day; *her* faith in Him was strong. . . but mine waned. She kept telling me that we would see Lazarus again, in the resurrection at the last day. I could not share her faith, so I sat at the house, but suddenly, Martha came up behind me and whispered in my ear, "The Master is calling for you." As soon as I heard that Jesus wanted to see me, I ran to Him; I desperately needed His comfort and to know the truth. When I arrived to where Jesus was, I fell to His feet weeping, saying, "Lord, if thou hadst been here, my brother had not died."[5] As we were all gathered in that place, just outside of town, Jesus asked where we had buried Lazarus. And then He did something I didn't expect. . . He cried. As *we* grieved and wept for Lazarus, Jesus wept *with* us.

Later, as we stood in front of the grave, Jesus asked to have the stone moved. We were shocked! Lazarus had been dead for four days already so Martha told Jesus that Lazarus would stink, yet Jesus told us that if we believed we would see the glory of God. So, we had the stone moved. Martha and I held each other as Jesus began to pray; we had no idea what was about to happen. Then Jesus called out to Lazarus in a loud voice, telling him to come out! We almost fainted! Much to our surprise, suddenly Lazarus came walking out, still bound with the grave clothes that we had put on him just a few days earlier. The joy that flooded our hearts and the praises that were given that day were amazing.

Jesus came back to our home one more time after that. We didn't know it then, but it was the last week of His life here on earth. Simon the Leper, His 12 disciples, Lazarus, Martha, and I all had supper together and as usual Martha was serving once again. This time, however, I noticed her attitude was different; she was serving from her heart, and it was beautiful to watch. I listened to the men talk to Jesus as He taught them, and my heart was just moved. They talked a lot about the religious leaders wanting to kill Him! I didn't know about that, but I did know this, those in authority did not want Jesus around after He raised Lazarus from the dead. In fact, we

---

[5] John 11:32 KJV

heard they wanted to kill our brother. After the men spoke, there was a heaviness about Jesus I hadn't seen before.

In those moments, my heart was so full of love for Jesus, I just knew I had to let Him know how much I loved Him and how thankful I was for Him in my life. I quietly got up and went into my sleeping area. I reached up onto the shelf where I had put my white alabaster box. I held it in my hands, feeling the combined weight of the box and the perfume it contained. I walked back to where Jesus was, broke the seal and poured the perfume over Him. As it dripped over His feet, I knelt down and wiped it with my hair; I prayed that my actions would convey the worship that my heart was feeling. Some of the men complained that I had been wasteful—that I should have sold the perfume for three hundred pence, or fifty dollars, and given it to the poor. I wasn't upset. Even Jesus told them to leave me alone; He said I was anointing Him for His time of burial.

It wasn't but fourteen days later when we heard that Jesus had been crucified. I wept like I had never wept before. My friend, the One who knew my innermost thoughts, the One who cried at the death of my brother, was dead. Yet, there was still this hope inside me that He too would rise from the dead, much like Lazarus. Three days later, we heard the news. Jesus had indeed, risen from the dead. My heart and soul could not contain the emotions, the praise, and the songs of worship that erupted from my heart.

*****************************************************************************************************

- Is there a difference between head worship and heart worship?

- What does worship look like, is there a right and wrong way to worship?

- When was the last time that you truly worshiped the Lord?

Mary's quilt square has to be the log cabin heart. The log cabin is a quilt square that is made of straight pieces of cloth that is sewn together in an "L" shape. Each added piece is a little longer than the one before, just like her love for Christ grew with each encounter.

I believe that each of us who have come to know Jesus as Savior was first drawn to Him in a special way that spoke only to us. Maybe it was a Sunday School story about how much He loved us, or it could have been a time when we felt all was lost. For each of us that starting point is different and yet we all have the same beginning. Like Mary our faith grows, perhaps through something we read about Him, a song we hear, or a sermon. Our hearts grow in love and worship, and when the bottom of our world falls out and the roof caves in, we turn to Him and find Him faithful. It is then that our worship moves from our head to our heart and like Mary and Martha, we give all that we have to Him.

# 8

# Rocks

## John 8:1-11 ~
## The Woman Caught in Adultery

There are some stories that are too painful to tell; the people involved are silent due to the part they have played along the way. The woman caught in adultery remains as silent as those who accused her. This story, therefore, is told from the viewpoint of a rock that witnessed the whole event.

"I was just lying around minding my own business when suddenly I was being pushed around. I was kicked aside just in time by someone's foot as a young woman's bare feet came crashing down on the other rocks around me. I couldn't see her face because her long dark hair covered it, but I could hear her weeping ever so softly. I watched as her tears silently and quickly fell to the ground, mingled with the dirt, and trickled toward me.

I saw the feet of many men, old and young, as they formed a circle. . . around the two of us. I had watched this scene play out many times before and I had no desire to be involved, yet I was as trapped as she was. Suddenly there were hands moving down toward the ground. I watched as smaller rocks were picked up and dropped. The words, "Too small," and "Not heavy enough," came crashing down with each rock that was tossed away.

Suddenly, I felt a smooth, barely calloused hand reach down to grab me; with a satisfied grunt I was enclosed in a sweaty palm. I could hear nothing and see even less, but then I started to be thrown up in the air. I hoped that I would be cast aside; I wanted nothing of what was to come, but that hope was quickly dashed as I was caught and thrown up again and again.

Each time I went up in the air, I could see the other rocks being tossed just as I was. Other men were still looking for the perfect stone. The young girl, still on her feet but now shaking with fear, was in the middle of the circle. About the fourth time I was thrown up in the air, I caught sight of something very strange; she was no longer alone. There was a man standing in the circle with her. He did not have a rock or intend on participating in what was about to happen.

Over the sounds of laughter and rocks hitting the palms of those assembled there, a man said, "Master, this woman was taken in adultery, in the very act. Now Moses in the law commanded us, that such should be stoned: but what sayest thou" (John 8:4-5 KJV)? As I went up in the air this time, I turned so I could get a good look at this "Master" the man had addressed. I knew the moment I saw His face that this was my Creator. I expected Him to speak and pass judgement on all, but instead, as I continued to be tossed up and down, I lost sight of Him. Surprised, I looked around the circle but did not see His face. Suddenly as I came down, I saw the top of His head. The Creator was bent down, writing on the ground. I could not see what He was writing but his finger was moving. I was confused by this action: the Creator of the universe—God Himself—bowing and writing in the dirt, when all He had to do was speak to end the oncoming tragedy.

The men continued questioning Him, each trying to out yell the other. Jesus acted as if He didn't hear them; the girl just kept watering the ground with her tears. The other rocks, going higher and higher, were smacking harder and harder into the hands of the men. I could feel the anger and tension building. I had a feeling it was not going to end well for either the girl, or my Creator. On my next trip upward, I watched Jesus stand and the men quieted down. He said, "He that is without sin among you, let him first cast a stone at her" (John 8:7 KJV).

I couldn't believe my ears! Did He not know He was speaking to a very self-righteous group of men, none of whom would ever admit they themselves had done anything wrong? I wondered, *what was He thinking*? Then I saw that He had bowed down again and was once more writing on the ground. I knew that at any minute arms would be drawn back and rocks would be flying into the flesh of that poor young girl, but the strangest thing happened. Had I not been there, I would have never believed it myself; the oldest man in the group dropped his stone and walked away without a word. I kept going up into the air but not as high and not with as much force as before. Slowly with each pass up, I saw more and more men dropping their rocks and walking away. Soon, only the young men were left. I was being held tightly and could barely hear the muffled sounds of the other rocks dropping with soft thuds to the ground. Suddenly, the sweaty hand that gripped me so tightly, began to uncurl its fingers and I, too, was released and hit the ground.

I rolled to the edge of the only garment that covered the young girl and watched as her feet disappeared. I peeked around the girl to see my Creator's finger still writing in the dirt. There was only silence left when Jesus rose and asked the girl, "Where are those thine accusers? Hath no man condemned thee" (John 8:10 KJV)? With a voice so soft I had to strain to hear, she replied, "No man, Lord." "Neither do I condemn thee: go and sin no more" (John 8:11 KJV).

Never had I seen such mercy, such love, and such grace which was bestowed on this young girl. If I could ever have cried out in complete worship of my God and Creator, it would have been then.

***********************************************************************************************************

- Have you felt the sting of condemnation?

- Has shame stopped you from using your voice?

- How do you think forgiveness changed the young woman's life?

- Could it change yours in the same way?

This woman's quilt square needs to be rocks. Rocks were to be used as judgement in this story, for her sin. Yet the rocks also signify the weight of shame she surely felt lifted from her shoulders when Jesus said He found no fault in her.

Shame. Such a powerfully negative word, yet when we do wrong, the shame or conviction we feel should lead us to repentance, not condemnation. Like the woman was told, we should go on our way, but sin no more.

Shame comes from many places: things that we have done, places we have been and if we are totally honest, things that have been done *to* us. Shame can come from people's judgment of us personally; this kind of shame makes us want to hide in the shadows. It quiets our voices and places condemnation on us like a neon light. When people judge and place shame on others, not knowing the whole story, to further their own agenda or help them to feel better about themselves, it is wrong. The weight of shame can take away our joy of living and diminish our ability to use the talents and gifts that God has given us.

The woman in this story felt ashamed to be sure, but she found her true worth in the words of Jesus. He does not place condemnation on us; He offers us love which leads to true freedom. We can find our true worth in Him, too. All we have to do is admit our sin, ask for forgiveness, then truly accept and believe that we are forgiven, and our sin is *forgotten*.

John 8:36 says, "If the Son makes you free, you shall be free indeed" (NKJV).

# 9

# Waves

Matt.9:20, Mark 25, Luke 8:43 ~
The Woman with the Issue of Blood


I watched from a distance as my family celebrated with yours, all the feasts of our God, as the seasons changed from planting to harvest. I watched as each year the Passover Lamb was chosen and the story of Moses and the deliverance of our people was recited. I listened to the songs of praise rise and carry through the night air to where I was—my voice joining yours. I watched as the children I knew grew up, and the boys completed the ceremony to become men in our faith. I longed to be a part of those ceremonies so badly, it hurt.

Then there were the funerals—so many friends and neighbors we knew—so many who I never had a chance to say goodbye to. Please know that when you rejoiced, I rejoiced with you and when your tears fell, and your wails of sorrow filled the air, I sorrowed with you. I wanted so much to be there that my heart broke to hold you, to wipe your tears away and to encourage you. Yet, we both know that according to the law I was unclean, unwanted, and unable to do anything to help myself.

Twelve years is a long time to be alone, to watch your life pass you by. It is a long time to be separated from your husband, children and friends. You need to know how desperate I was to do what I did; I just wanted someone to touch me again—a hug, a pat on the arm, to feel the arms of a little one around my neck. I wanted to pet an animal, meet my friends in the marketplace to laugh with them or share a recipe. I wanted to be a mother, wife, and daughter again, and end the loneliness that I was feeling. I couldn't face another night of crying myself to sleep; I was tired of not really living.

I had overheard from the women passing by that there was this man called Jesus—that He had been born in a town much like ours. The story went that He was the Son of God, the One that had been promised to our father, Abraham, and that He was to be our Redeemer, but I had also heard that He was hated by the Sadducees and the Pharisees, the ones who enforced the laws of our faith. They were the ones that had put me where I am, but I did not hate them for that. I knew that they were just following the law of Moses.

There was also much talk that this man, our Redeemer called Jesus, had been healing people. I know! I could hardly believe it myself, but there was proof; the nobleman's son was alive, and Peter's mother-in-law had been healed. Remember the man with the withered hand, the one who stood outside the temple? He could never straighten it out, yet the other day he walked by, and I saw with my own eyes his hand strong and straight. I saw that he, once again, could enter the temple to pray with the men. The word on the street is that Jesus healed him just by speaking.

Others have been healed as well. He must be the Son of God because just the other day there was such an uproar on the street. People were talking about the disciples and Jesus being in a boat when a huge storm came up; Jesus was asleep in the boat when the disciples woke Him up because they were so scared, even as fishermen. His disciples had been out in storms before, nevertheless, there was something terrible and frightening about this one. The story goes that Jesus stood up and commanded the winds and the waves to stop and they did!

I thought all hope was gone for me since it had been twelve long, lonely years. I had spent all my money on cures that did nothing for me. I had honestly asked forgiveness for every sin I could think of and made many offerings at the temple, to no avail. The sickness was bad enough but the judgment of others and their comments about my sins were worse. What hurt most and truly broke my heart and spirit, were the rumors about what sin I must have committed to be punished this way, especially when those who gossiped, I counted as friends. *What did I have to lose?* I thought, *no one talked to me anyway*. I knew I was going to die from this condition.

I started listening to what others were saying, to know when this Jesus was coming to visit our temple. I knew that I knew, He was my last and only chance, so when I again overheard that He was headed to our town, I changed my clothes and waited. I heard a commotion in the streets as He entered our little town and the hope inside me soared, *If only! If only I could touch Him!*

I stood in my doorway hoping He would notice me, but then I realized that there was no way He would ever be able to see me through the crowd. I stepped out of my doorway and waited for someone to say something, but nobody did, so I started making my way through the crowd, crouching low as to not be seen. I was crouching so low that I might as well have been crawling on my hands and knees. My only thought was, *if only I could get close enough to touch His robe, I would be healed*.

He came closer—there was a huge crowd around Him. I slowly pushed my way in and just as He passed by, I reached out my hand and touched the tassels that hung off His garment—the very tassels that reminded everyone of the commandment that made me and anyone that came into contact with me, unclean. I felt power rush through my body; my strength was instantly renewed, and peace and joy filled my heart like it never had before at the relief I felt in my body.

Unfortunately, the joy was short lived when I heard Him ask who had touched Him. The crowd became silent. The disciples told Him that because there were so many people around, anyone could have touched Him. But He looked around. I could almost feel His eyes searching for me; I knew I had to confess. I stood up. That is when I saw the looks of shock on the faces of you, my friends, who knew my story. Your condemning looks said it all. I slowly turned my head toward the One whom I had touched, expecting the same look of condemnation. I straightened up a little taller, turned toward Him and with my eyes to the ground, I quietly admitted what I had done. I expected the same condemnation that you, my friends, had given me, yet instead, He said that my faith had made me whole. That alone would have been enough for me but as I looked at Him now, I saw only unconditional love and acceptance in His eyes. I was overcome! Falling to my knees with tears flowing freely down my face, I worshipped Jesus, my Lord, with all my heart. There were no words to tell of my complete joy and peace as I realized that I was free to join my family, walk in the marketplace, and worship with my friends and family. I had been healed and made whole!

John 10:10 says, "I have come that they may have life, and that they may have it more abundantly" (NKJV).

***********************************************************************************************************

The woman with the issue of blood was declared unclean by the law and faced rejection and even death for her touch. She had to humble herself to the point of reaching out to touch the bottom of His garment in total desperation—her very last hope. Are you there? Are you worn out from trying to make things work, never getting it quite right? What is holding you back from being able to fulfill what God has planned for you?

No, it won't be easy. It may be risky, and it may take some work to be healed, but do it anyway. Reach out to Jesus! Let Him know about your desperation, your pain, loneliness, sorrows and fears. Let Him heal you from your emotional damage, from the sin of unforgiveness, and perhaps the guilt that you have been carrying around. Never mind what everyone else will think of you and reach out in faith; touch the only One who can heal you just as she did. Then you will see what she saw—the look of unconditional love and acceptance in the face of your Redeemer.

- Do you desire to be healed?

- What is your desire to be healed from?

- How will your healing change you?

- What will it take for you to take that step of faith?

This woman's quilt square is called *Waves*. It is fitting for her as the waves of embarrassment and shame would have overwhelmed her each time she had to called out, unclean. Those same waves would have washed over her each time she listened to the opinions of others about how her sin caused her issue. Yet more than anything, the waves of embarrassment and shame had to be overwhelming when she had to stand up in front of everyone and confess what she had done. Thankfully, those shameful waves soon turned into waves of pure joy and worship when Jesus told her that her faith had made her whole.

# 10

# Annie's Choice

Luke 13:11-16 ~
The Woman Bowed Over

I remember feeling the sun on my face, running through town and playing with my sisters and girlfriends. The carefree days of my youth were spent traveling up and down these streets, looking into the stalls on market day to examine all they had to offer. I remember the smells of fresh cooked items and the feel of different textures of cloth between my fingers. I remember how the sun made jewelry sparkle and how it sent rainbows dancing across my hands. I would see a young man looking my way and give him a shy smile, then turn away. Friends and relatives would meet to catch up on the news and their laughter filled the air. And the music! How I loved to dance and clap as it filled the streets.

I remember lying on the rooftop of our home at night and looking up into the sky where stars sparkled like diamonds. Then there was the moon, so big and bright I often thought that if I tried hard enough, I could reach up and touch it. Yet despite all that loveliness surrounding me, our synagogue was my favorite place to be. During our weekly visits I listened attentively as men read the word of God, and I looked in wonder at all the beautiful designs and colors around me.

For the last eighteen years, however, my days have consisted of looking at the ground. I see feet—lots of feet. I can tell who someone is by his or her feet and choice of sandal. These days, most people walk right by me in the market, their eyes searching for the right stalls where they can buy different foods and other necessities. Perhaps they're just enjoying a glorious day, feeling the sun beaming its warmth into them, or perhaps searching for the familiar face of a friend, or a loved one in the crowd. Sometimes people bump into me, and yell at me as if I've done something wrong. There are some who tell me I have no right to be around them—that when I approach people, I should be hollering, "Unclean!" like lepers are required to do. There are those who believe and announce whenever they see me, that I have sinned, and this infirmity is proof. They believe that if I confess my sin, I will be healed. Others, mostly the younger ones, call me names and mimic me. It is not my fault I am bowed over and cannot stand up straight! The doctors don't know what caused it or how to fix it, so I just keep doing what I need to do to live a life that pleases God.

Some of my friends are surprised that I'm not bitter or angry with God for allowing this to happen. The thought of *that* simply astounds me! Why in the world would I be bitter about what's happened to me? Am I not still alive? I can still get around, even though admittedly, the pain is sometimes unbearable. I can still listen to my friends and family speak and be a part of great conversations. As far as the market goes, as long as nobody switches the stalls around, I still know what each one sells. And whenever things get hard, I can close my eyes and remember how the sun felt on my face, and how stars shimmer in the night sky.

No one can be angry with God and love Him at the same time. If I truly believe that Jevovah is my Creator and in control of all that happens to me, then I <u>must</u> believe with my whole heart that this infirmity is His will. But please don't think of me as a saint! I have days when my pain is so bad, I can barely move. There are days when my tears could fill a pail and times when I completely and honestly feel sorry for myself. I want to stand tall and look people in the eye instead of at their feet. I want to hold a newborn, lift my face to the sun and wear the latest colors. Yet this is the path I must walk, so I shall. I know that if it is Jehovah's will, I will stand tall again. Until then, I will not be bitter or angry, though perhaps just a little sad some days. No matter what, I have resolved in my heart not to become a bitter, angry woman. I will continue to praise my Creator and my God as long as I live.

*****************

Today I must leave my home extra early. It's the Sabbath, my favorite day of the whole week, and I am going to the synagogue. I love to listen to the music and the hum of people's voices as we pass each other. This is the day that is set aside—no work or marketing may be done. Today, I'll worship with my family and friends. As I travel down the road, I notice there are a lot more people than usual. They're rushing and they seem excited about something—or perhaps someone, but no one will stop long enough to tell me what's going on.

When I get inside, I take my usual spot, close enough to hear, but not to draw attention to myself. The room quiets down, and I hear a voice I've never heard before. This teacher speaks with an air of authority and knowledge, yet there's something else in His voice, a sense of urgency mixed with love for the people gathered before him. I sit listening and my heart fills with worship. I become unaware of anyone else around me.

Suddenly, I hear the teacher calling me to come to Him. I shake my head in disbelief; he must want someone else! Why would He want me to come to Him? I wonder if He'll call me out for being there—if He thinks I have sinned—if He too, judges me? I see the feet of those around me part as a path opens up. I'm filled with dread but what choice do I have? I stand up on my feet, straighten my clothes and with eyes cast to the ground, I start to walk forward. Never in my life has time passed so slowly. The crowd is silent, as if they are awaiting my condemnation. I must admit, I am in total fear, but if the truth be known, there is something about Him that makes me feel completely loved—just as I am. I stand bowed before Him and hear Him say, "Woman, thou art loosed from thine infirmity" (Luke 13:12 KJV).  Then He lays His hands on me, and immediately I stand up, my spine flexible and straight—all my pain, gone!

Oh, what utter joy for the first person I look in the eye in eighteen years is Jesus, the Son of God, my Creator! I begin to worship and glorify God, raising my voice in praise, my feet dancing with joy because I cannot keep them still!  Tears flow down my face. It does not matter what anyone else thinks or says, I am healed by the grace of God, and I am praising Him with everything I have that I can possibly give Him.

All my life, I have believed in God's word about His promised Savior and trusted in the One unseen. But now, I have seen Him, face to face.  I have seen living proof of God's promise to His people. I have seen Jesus Himself.

For as long as I live, I will praise Him and adore Him.

*************************************************************************************************************

Although this woman had every right to be bitter and angry, she chose to worship God instead. The key word here is, *chose*. Every day, we make many choices, and among those choices, we choose how we will see the world. Some people do choose bitterness and anger; they become resentful toward God, with other people, and with the world in general. They say life isn't fair. To them, the only way to view life is with bitterness and anger, but that doesn't change their circumstances. It changes them.

The truth is life is <u>not</u> fair. If it were, Jesus would never have had to die on the cross to pay for our sins and each of us would have to pay for his or her own iniquities.

************************************************************************************************************

This woman's quilt square is called *Annie's Choice.* She had to make a decision; she could become bitter and angry, or demand that people wait on her. She could have turned her back on God. She could have spent the rest of her life complaining all day long about how unfair her life was. Instead, she chose to worship the Lord, her Creator. This story, found in Luke 13, says she was in the synagogue that day, but not because Jesus was there. He saw her, but from her bowed position, she could not see Him. When He called her to Him, she chose to trust Him, to obey Him and to continue strengthening her faith in Him.

Today <u>you</u> have a choice:  bitterness and anger, or thanksgiving and praise. He is calling for <u>you</u> to come forward and waiting with His hands outstretched for your response.

- If you have chosen bitterness and anger, how far have they gotten you?

- Who are you angry at, really? People? Yourself? Your circumstances? Or Jesus?

If you're tired of having bitterness and anger fill your heart and you want to go forward with thanksgiving and praise instead, simply choose it, and realize that your circumstances may not change—but <u>you</u> surely will.

# 11

# Tears

## Matt 26: 7, Mark 14:3, Luke 7:37 ~
## The Woman with the Alabaster Box

I have been walking these streets for years. I no longer hide my face from people's stares as I have in the past; they know who I am and what I do, so why bother. This is not how I expected my life to turn out. My father had great hopes for me to marry and produce grandsons—grandsons to whom he could teach our faith and give him bragging rights at the wall where the men gather. Now when he sees me, he turns his head away as if someone or something has caught his attention. In reality, we both know what the truth is; he is ashamed of me and what I do.

I wish I could tell you how it all started but I have long erased that memory from my mind. I am not happy with how life turned out for me, that is for certain. I am so tired of being put down by the women around here, who think they are better than I am. I see them purposely turning their backs on me when I approach the market, then step aside if I get too close. Behind their raised hands I can hear what they are saying about me. My heart breaks every time it happens.

These were my childhood friends; we used to spend every minute we could together. Can't they see that some choices are made for you and are not yours to make?

The men are no better. Those who share my bed, talk, and laugh with me privately, but out in public they look down their pious noses at me, as if I'm trash. When I ask them about it when we're alone, they tell me they really don't mean it. . . but I know the truth. I am unlovable, unwanted, and not worthy of anyone's time and space. Some days I am so lonely, I just want to die.

Even with being treated like an outcast by others, I think even worse is the fact that I can't join my family in any of our faith celebrations. Although, if I'm honest, I'm not even sure I believe any more, or if I want to. Some of the men who visit me in my home are the same men that stand in the temple and worship as if their hands are not dirty with the same sin they accuse me of.

This afternoon there was an uproar at the gate of our town; people were running down the street claiming that they had seen Jesus. He is from a little town called Nazareth. His father was a carpenter but there is something different about Him. Some say He's the Son of God Almighty. Just the other day, He healed a man in the temple who had a withered hand. He didn't even touch the man; Jesus only spoke, and the man's hand was normal. Personally though, I would not have been interested in Jesus at all, had it not been for another woman I heard about. This woman had been sick for a long time and she, much like me, was considered unclean. Jesus was walking down the road and she dared to reach out and touch the bottom of His garment; immediately she was healed and not condemned.

Jesus is here in our town and people have been running up and down the roads telling everyone about Him. It seems there was a man in our town who had a servant who was sick, and this man asked Jesus to heal his servant. The servant was completely healed! Then I watched from a distance as Jesus raised the widow's son from a funeral pyre. I heard Him when

He spoke to John's disciples saying, "Blessed is he, whosoever shall not be offended in me" (Matthew 11:6 KJV). I didn't understand a lot of what He was saying, but those words struck a chord deep down inside me; I knew what it was like to be an offense to everyone I met. I wondered why anyone would be offended in Him. Jesus an offense? This man who loved the people that the Pharisees and Sadducees could not love? Jesus who healed the sick, raised the dead and was not afraid of being around sinners? One could see the love in His eyes as He looked around at the people. No, He was no offense. When He looked my way, I felt that I had been seen—really seen, for who I was and not for what I did. I felt. . . dare I say. . . loved—such a long-forgotten feeling. I felt loved and important to Him; it was like I really mattered to Him.

I had not felt loved by anyone for so long and I knew I just had to express my love for *Him* in return, somehow. I wasn't sure what to do until I heard Simon the Pharisee invite Jesus to his house for a meal. Jesus would recline at the table and be there for quite some time, so I went home and took the alabaster box off the shelf in my bedroom. It contained the ointment that I had bought to have my body anointed in after I died. (I was smart enough to know that nobody else would care enough to buy it for me.) I walked to Simon's home and walked right in as if I belonged there. The men were in deep conversation. Simon must have seen me coming, but he said nothing. I was too ashamed to look at Jesus in the eye and too afraid of being condemned, so I approached Jesus from behind; I don't believe He even heard me coming.

Love overwhelmed my heart as I fell at His feet; tears poured from my eyes. I took my long auburn hair, the symbol of my glory, down from its clip and as my tears wet His feet, I wiped them dry with my hair. Then, I kissed His feet—the feet of the man who had brought healing and love to so many people, but I wasn't done yet. The white marble box felt cool to my touch as I broke open the seal of wax; the smell of the anointing oil began to fill the room. I poured the perfume out onto His feet, anointing them.

I lingered there, enjoying His presence, laying at His feet and as I did, I heard Jesus start to speak to Simon. He talked about two people who owed money to a creditor; one person owed five hundred pence and the other five. Jesus went on to say that when the creditor realized that neither of them could pay, the creditor forgave them both. Then He asked Simeon this question, "Which one of them will love him more?" Simon did not even have to think. Simon replied that the man who was forgiven the most would love the creditor more and Jesus told him he was right.

I wasn't sure why Jesus was telling this story, but He continued. He stated that Simon had not washed His feet when He entered the house, yet I had washed His feet with my tears and dried them with my hair. Jesus also pointed out that Simon had not greeted Him with a kiss, yet I had not stopped kissing His feet. Then Jesus finished and said that Simon had not anointed His head with oil, but I had anointed His feet. When He was done, Jesus looked at *me* and spoke what I desperately needed to hear. Jesus told me that my sins were forgiven, and I could go in peace because my faith had saved me. I was amazed He would even acknowledge me. He knew me and what I needed even though I had asked for nothing from Him. My desire was just to worship Him, but instead I was given everything: my life, self-worth, and a chance to start all over again. I was no longer the harlot. I was forgiven and more importantly, LOVED by Jesus. With my head held high I left Simon's home. I walked down the street and looked people right in the eye. I was not condemned, in turmoil or excluded any more. Jesus Christ had forgiven me and it did not matter what other people thought of me anymore. I was known and loved. I would follow Him for the rest of my life.

*************************************************************************************************************

- Have you ever felt unworthy?

- What does worship look like to you?

- When was the last time you worshipped from your heart

Each of us, who have come to know Jesus as Savior, was given the same thing as this woman. . . our pasts wiped clean. How has that changed you?

Simon was a Pharisee, a member of an ancient Jewish sect, who had memorized the first five books of the Old Testament, called the Torah. He believed in strict obedience to the law handed down by God to Moses, as well as traditional law. Simon would have thought himself to be above all the other people around him; some might say he was self-righteous. The nameless woman, on the other hand, was a harlot. She had led an imperfect life and did not know the law fully; she would not have memorized any part of the Torah, let alone a single verse. Quite a difference in people wouldn't you say? Yet their status was not what Jesus was looking at—it was their hearts. Simon gave nothing to Jesus aside from a meal, but the woman gave everything. Simon may have just wanted the prestige of having Jesus at his house.

The woman never spoke, but her actions spoke volumes. She was drawn to Him, to His words of love which brought forth worship, reverent honor, humility, tears, wiping His feet with her hair and kissing them which equated to *pure* worship from the heart. When was the last time you worshipped from your heart? The quilt square to represent her must be *Tears of Worship*.

Psalm 86:12 says, "I give thanks to you, O Lord my God, with my whole heart, and I will glorify your name forever" (ESV).

# 12

# Cross with a Heart

## Luke 8 ~ Mary Magdalene

All I wanted was for someone to see past not only my wealth but also the burden that I carried; I wanted someone to love and accept me as I was. My burden you ask? Let me introduce myself to you. I am Mary from Magdalene and now I am sure that you know the burden that I carried. I was possessed.

Let's be honest here. Over time, lots of money was thrown at many doctors and spent on many strange and exotic treatments, but my burden was never healed. I was in utter despair. So, when I heard that there was this man, Jesus, and He had healed others, I had to go find Him. I thought if I got close enough maybe I could offer Him some money and He would heal me too. I just wanted to be normal. . . to have a family and live like everyone else, so I went looking and there He was.

I stood in the crowd listening to Him teach; He talked about things that I had never heard of before. As I listened, it started to get late and I thought if I didn't move soon, He would be gone, and I would have lost my chance. So, I moved into His line of sight. I will never forget the first time He looked at me; it was as if a shadow of sorrow passed quickly over His face. I thought I had offended Him, so I started to walk away. My mind raced with dismay. Surely, He was no different than anyone else. What in the world was I thinking coming here?

Then I heard my name. "Mary," He said to me and as I turned, His arms were outstretched in my direction. I hesitated, glancing around furtively at His disciples and the others in the crowd who were standing there watching. I looked at His face and saw acceptance. But wait! There was something more. It was like He could see right through me, past what I looked like on the outside, to who I really was in the very depth of my soul. He called my name again and I ran to Him, dropping at His feet with my head to the ground. I felt His hands on my head and then the most amazing thing happened. I can't really explain it; it was as if I was suddenly set free, not on the outside but on the inside! Tears fell from my eyes as He lifted me to my feet. I once again looked into His eyes and saw pure love and acceptance. His next words to me were, "You are healed."

Suddenly, my life was changed. No longer was anything else as important to me; I just wanted to serve my Lord with all that I had. I met up with Jesus' mother Mary and Joanna that day. I began to help them minister to His needs with my money, time and talents. Life was great as I sat under His teaching and learned to love Him more each day.

One day, He went into Jerusalem riding on a donkey. Oh, you should have seen it! People were shouting, "Hosanna, blessed be the King of Israel that cometh in the name of the Lord." Children were dancing and coats and palm branches were being strewn on the ground before Him. It appeared they had learned to love Him as much as I did, but then, in a matter of days, life as I knew it stopped.

Somehow, Jesus went from being praised in the street to being hated and even wanted by the Romans. Soldiers arrested Him in the Garden of Gethsemane. He was taken before

Pilate, and He was brutally beaten. I stood in the crowd of people when Pilate, according to custom, asked which prisoner should go free. I couldn't believe my ears when the people cried out for Barabbas to be set free instead of Jesus. Those around me hollered for Jesus to be crucified. Were these not the same people who had cried out Hosanna just a few days ago? What had happened to their announcement that He came in the name of the Lord? This had to be a nightmare, but even though I tried, I couldn't wake myself up.

I followed behind the men as they climbed the mount where they would crucify my Lord. I had never felt so helpless; there was nothing I could do. I heard the hammers hitting the nails and the thud of the cross being dropped into the ground. The whole time, the crowd was laughing and jeering.

I didn't want to look, but I had no choice. He needed to know that I still loved Him, that I was there, and still believed in Him. I couldn't do anything to help Him; my money meant nothing at that point, but I was there. Slowly, I lifted my eyes as unashamed tears fell and my heart ripped into pieces. This man who had only done good, who healed and loved was beaten, bruised and bloodied so much that I barely recognized Him. I looked into His eyes as if to *will* Him to know how much I loved Him. I stood there with His mother, and I heard every word He said. When He cried out, "It is finished," I cried out, "This can't be the end! What will we do without You?"

They came and took His body down; I followed to see where they would bury Him. When they were gone and I was alone, I fell face first to the ground and cried as I had never cried before. The One who loved me in a way that no one else ever could, was gone. I was devastated.

The first of the week came and I returned to where they left Him. I rose early, leaving before dawn as I wanted to be there at sunrise. I carried all the spices I would need to anoint His body according to our traditions. If there was nothing else I could do, I could at least do this. As

I approached the tomb, I noticed that something was wrong. The stone covering the entrance had been moved. I entered the tomb and saw that the body of Jesus was gone.

How could this be? Where had they taken Him? What was happening? I ran as fast as I could and told Peter what had happened. We ran back to the garden and Peter looked in but left immediately. Alone, I stood outside weeping; I couldn't make myself leave. Jesus had been my healer, my friend and my Lord. When my tears had eased, I once again looked into the tomb, as if by chance His body would be there, but instead of His body, I saw two angels. They asked me why I was crying, so I told them that I didn't know where they had taken my Lord. As I stood there, I felt a presence I hadn't felt moments earlier, so I turned. Immediately, I saw a man standing there; I thought he was the gardener. He asked me why I was crying, but I insisted to know where they had taken Jesus. I desperately wanted to honor Him by preparing His body for burial.

Then I heard my name, "Mary." My breath stopped. Time stood still. Only once before had I heard my name spoken with so much compassion and love. Could it be? Yes, I knew it was. I would know His voice anywhere. Jesus, my Master and Lord, stood before me, alive! I was never so happy to see anyone before!

Jesus instructed me to go and tell the disciples that He had risen from the dead, so I ran. I ran as fast as my legs would carry me, ready to share the good news that Jesus Christ was alive! My Lord spent another forty days on the earth (some of which we enjoyed with Him) before He finally went up into the clouds—to be with His Father, He said. Even though I could no longer see Him, I knew He was alive and I spent the rest of my life serving the One who loved me so much that He died for me. How could I do less?

******************************************************************************************************

Mary Magdalene's quilt square needs to be called *The Healing Heart*. Only a broken heart, who has met the Savior of the world, can be healed. Thus, Mary's heart was completely healed by her Savior and as a result, she was able to serve Him with open and inviting arms—for she understood His love for her and the world.

*************************************************************************************************

I heard someone say that we will never understand the love that Christ has for us. I was not surprised that at the next communion service, this thought came into my mind, *if I really understood how much He loved me, in what ways would my life be different?* Mary Magdalene understood that love; she saw it personally as He hung on the cross and died for her and us. Personally, I know that I love Him, but in all honesty, some of that *awe* I first felt when I initially met Him, when I learned that He loved me so much He died for me, has faded over time. It has been replaced with concerns and burdens of this world and things I need to change in my life.

I also began to wonder, *if I truly understood how much He loved me, wouldn't I trust Him completely with everything and everyone I love? If I understood His love for me, wouldn't I rest completely in the knowledge that He has my life, my needs and my future in His hands? If I understood His love for me, wouldn't I use my gifts to honor Him regardless of how scared or incompetent I feel? Wouldn't I be able to stand on His promises when everything is falling around me? Wouldn't I, if I truly understood, the length, the depth and the width of His love for me, be able, like Mary, to give Him all of me to use as He sees fit? No matter the consequences, the gains, or the losses?* Then I began to wonder why I would wait until I understood His love *completely* before I started to act like I believed it. For it is only when we acknowledge how much He loves us that we are free to serve Him with all we have and let Him to take care of the rest.

- What is holding you back from believing that Jesus loves you?

- What changes would it make in your life if you truly believed that Jesus loved you?

- How has your life changed since you asked Him into your life?

Jeremiah 31:3 says, "I have loved thee with an everlasting love: therefore with lovingkindness have I drawn thee."

# ABOUT THE AUTHOR

Susan Peaslee is a graduate of Glen Cove Bible College. She grew up in Wells, Maine, and now resides in Somerville, Maine. She and her husband Neil have been married 44 years, have three sons, two daughters and 14 grandchildren. She has been involved in VBS at her church for 42 years and in women's ministry for more than 30 years. Susan works as an Ed Tech III in a local public school. She is a writer and speaker who loves to study the Word of God. Her heart has been broken through loss and healed by her Savior's love. She desires to help other women heal from their brokenness and to feel the closeness of God. She is passionate about the power of prayer. Susan loves to quilt, read and sit by the ocean.